W9-AEW-867

Welcome to ALADDIN QUIX!

If you are looking for fast, fun-to-read stories with colorful characters, lots of kid-friendly humor, easy-to-follow action, entertaining story lines, and lively illustrations, then **ALADDIN QUIX** is for you!

But wait, there's more!

If you're also looking for stories with tables of contents; word lists; about-the-book questions; 64, 80, or 96 pages; short chapters; short paragraphs; and large fonts, then **ALADDIN QUIX** is *definitely* for you!

ALADDIN QUIX: The next step between ready to reads and longer, more challenging chapter books, for readers five to eight years old.

Read more ALADDIN QUIX books!

Our Principal Is a Frog!
by Stephanie Calmenson

Our Principal Is a Wolf!
by Stephanie Calmenson

Royal Sweets 1: A Royal Rescue
by Helen Perelman

Royal Sweets 2: Sugar Secrets
by Helen Perelman

A Miss Mallard Mystery: Texas Trail to Calamity
by Robert Quackenbush

A Miss Mallard Mystery: Dig to Disaster
by Robert Quackenbush

A Miss Mallard Mystery: Express Train to Trouble
by Robert Quackenbush

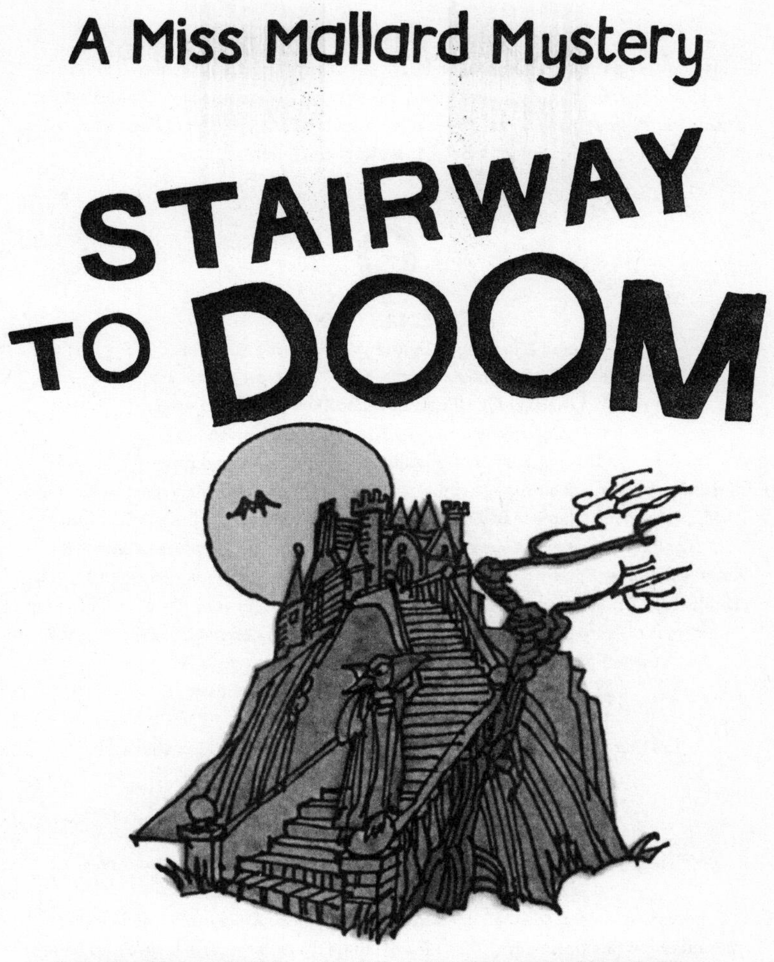

ROBERT QUACKENBUSH

New York London Toronto Sydney New Delhi

ALADDIN QUIX
Simon & Schuster Children's Publishing Division
1230 Avenue of the Americas, New York, New York 10020
This Aladdin QUIX hardcover edition September 2018

Also available in an Aladdin QUIX paperback edition.

Series and jacket designed by Nina Simoneaux
Interior designed by Tiara Iandiorio
The illustrations for this book were rendered in pen and ink and wash.
The text of this book was set in Archer Medium.
Manufactured in the United States of America 0818 FFG
2 4 6 8 10 9 7 5 3 1
The Library of Congress has cataloged a previous edition as follows:
Quackenbush, Robert M. / Stairway to doom
Summary: As one of thirteen guests invited to historic Duckinbill Castle to hear the will of her late great-aunt, Miss Mallard finds the other guests have disappeared overnight and it is up to her to solve the mystery.
[1. Ducks—Fiction. 2. Mystery and detective stories.] I. Title.
PZ7.Q16St 1983 [Fic] 82-21484
ISBN 978-1-5344-1316-0 (hc)
ISBN 978-1-5344-1315-3 (pbk)
ISBN 978-1-5344-1317-7 (eBook)

First for Piet, who told me about Kisscula,

and now for Emma and Aidan

Cast of Characters

Miss Mallard: World-famous ducktective

Inspector Willard Widgeon: Miss Mallard's nephew and inspector with the Swiss police

Effie: Relative of Abigail Spoonbill

Mario Sprig: Lawyer in charge of reading the will of Abigail Spoonbill

Abigail Spoonbill: Also known as Great Aunt Abby, recently deceased owner of Duckinbill Castle, whose will is being read

Jillie, Millie, and Tillie Butterball: Sisters, and relatives of Abigail Spoonbill

Count Kisscula: A kisspire who is said to haunt Duckinbill Castle

Josie and Amy Eider: Sisters, and relatives of Abigail Spoonbill

George and Bernard Scaup: Brothers, and relatives of Abigail Spoonbill

Bill, Bob, and Jim Teal: Brothers, and relatives of Abigail Spoonbill

What's in Miss Mallard's Bag?

Miss Mallard has many detective tools she brings with her on her adventures around the world.

In her knitting bag she usually has:

- Newspaper clippings
- Knitting needles and yarn
- A magnifying glass
- A flashlight
- A mirror
- A travel guide
- Chocolates for her nephew

Contents

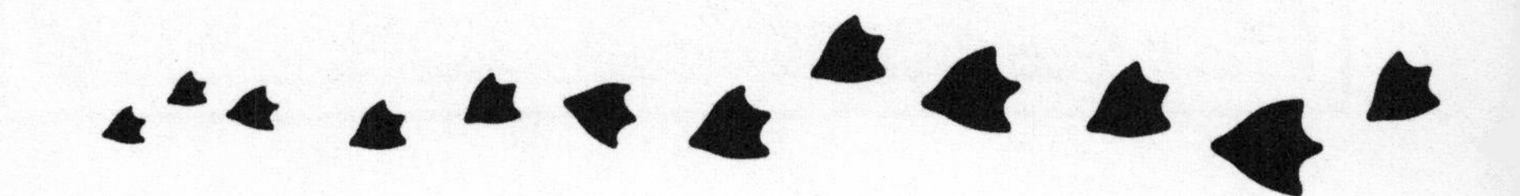

A Stormy Night

A flash of lightning ripped across the night sky. **Miss Mallard**, the world-famous ducktective, paid the carriage driver and hurried up the stairway that led to Duckinbill Castle.

Lightning struck again, and there was a crash of thunder.

"Stop that!" Miss Mallard quacked at the sky. "You act as if doom awaits me at the castle, not a simple reading of a will!"

Miss Mallard came to the front entrance of the castle. She rapped a rusty iron **knocker** against the heavy wooden door.

Inspector Willard Widgeon of the Swiss police, and Miss Mallard's nephew, opened the door.

"I knew it would be you, Aunty," he said. "That's why I answered the door. **Come in!** How good to see you again!"

"It's good to see you again too, Willard," said Miss Mallard. "I'm glad you were able to get away from your work and come to Scotland. Am I the last to arrive?"

"Yes," answered Inspector Widgeon. He hung Miss Mallard's umbrella on the crowded umbrella rack.

"Oh my!" said Miss Mallard.

"That makes me the thirteenth relative, my lucky number!"

"Twelfth now," said Inspector Widgeon. "First cousin twice removed **Effie** has disappeared. But she'll turn up, I'm sure. It's easy to get lost in this creepy old place with its dark passageways and winding halls."

He continued, "Come, let's join the others. The lawyer, **Mario Sprig**, is about to read the will."

They went into the main hall and sat down.

"Shall we begin?" said Mario Sprig. "You have all been asked here because you are the last surviving relatives of **Abigail Spoonbill**, known to many of you as Great Aunt Abby."

He went on, "She owned this castle. Her will states you must stay in the castle for *one* night. Those who do will **inherit** a share of the castle. But the will ends with a warning. It says,

"'BEWARE OF KISSCULA.'"

2

Haunted Castle

Mario Sprig snapped his brief-case shut and got up to leave.

"But who is Kisscula?" **Jillie, Millie, and Tillie Butterball** asked.

Mario Sprig answered, "I believe this castle was once the

home of **Count Kisscula**, a terrible kisspire. He hunted for victims to kiss when the moon was full. And you know how we ducks hate to be kissed!"

Everyone gasped when Sprig said, "It is believed his ghost haunts the castle. In fact, I think your cousin Effie knew this. Perhaps she was afraid to stay the night."

Sprig turned away. "Well, I must be going," he called. "My carriage is waiting. I have to

catch a ship back to Italy for my **culinary** class."

The door banged shut, and the noise echoed throughout the castle, making everyone shiver. Then a sudden roar of thunder outside made them jump with fright.

"**Infernal** thunderbolt!" Inspector Widgeon quacked.

Miss Mallard stood on the landing and said, "It will end soon."

And then she asked, "Are we

all staying tonight—ghost or no ghost?"

There was no reply.

"Good!" said Miss Mallard. "Then I suggest that we all find rooms and turn in for the night. Do keep an eye out for Cousin Effie. Maybe she is hiding somewhere."

Everyone grabbed candles and went upstairs.

Inspector Widgeon assigned rooms to all the relatives.

"Aunty, you can take the fifth

bedroom," said the inspector. "And Cousin Effie can sleep in your room if she reappears. I'll be in the maid's room next to Aunty's room."

"Fine," said Miss Mallard.

They all went to their rooms and lay down on **ancient** beds.

The lightning and thunder stopped.

The sky began to clear and **revealed** twinkling stars.

But there was a full moon!

In their bedrooms everyone slept soundly.

But for how long?

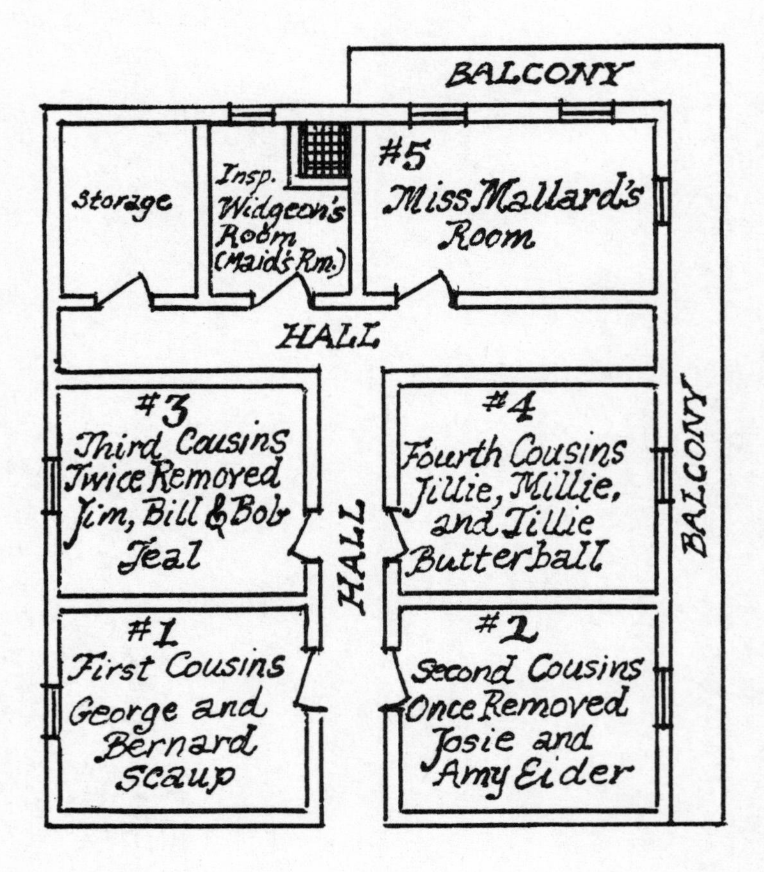

3

Midnight Quacks

Ding! A clock downstairs chimed twelve times. It was midnight. Suddenly **ear-piercing** quacks could be heard. Everyone ran out into the hall.

"The quacks are coming from

Josie and Amy Eider's room!" said **George and Bernard Scaup.**

Everyone ran to the second bedroom door. **It was locked!**

Bill, Bob, and Jim Teal hurled themselves against the sisters' door. It gave way, and the brothers fell into the room.

Everyone saw Amy and Josie passed out cold on the floor.

The **commotion** revived the Eider sisters.

"Horrors! Horrors!" they quacked. "We saw the kisspire! He

was trying to get into our room from the balcony!"

"Are you saying that you saw the ghost of Count Kisscula?" asked Inspector Widgeon.

"It wasn't a ghost," cried Josie. "He was real. Our quacks scared him away."

"Thank goodness for that!" said Miss Mallard. "Did you see his face?"

"No," sobbed Amy. "It was covered by the high collar of his long black cape."

"We want to go home!" wailed the Eider sisters together.

"Be calm," said Miss Mallard. "I am sure there is a reasonable explanation for this."

"You must stay!" said Inspector Widgeon. "You will lose your share of the **estate** if you don't. And after all, as Aunty said, this will all be over by morning."

"Well, all right," said Josie.

Amy said, "But believe me, we are going to prop heavy furniture

against all our doors and windows."

"Good idea," said Inspector Widgeon. "Everyone should do the same."

They all went back to their rooms, and the castle was quiet again.

A Basket of Garlic

Ding! Ding!

The clock struck two.

Miss Mallard heard someone knocking at her nephew's door. She jumped out of bed and moved a chest away from her own door.

Miss Mallard peeked out into the hall.

She saw Inspector Widgeon talking to Bill and Bob Teal.

"What's the trouble?" she asked.

Inspector Widgeon answered, "Bill and Bob say that their brother Jim has disappeared."

"Yes," said Bill. "Jim couldn't sleep. He said he was going to the library for a book. **He's not afraid of anything!** He left an hour ago and hasn't returned."

"Have you been down to the

library?" asked Miss Mallard.

"Are you kidding?" said Bill. "Jim may like living dangerously, but we don't. We were wondering if the inspector would go."

"Very well!" said Inspector Widgeon. "Return to your room. I'll investigate."

"I'll go with you, Willard," said Miss Mallard.

She grabbed a flashlight from her knitting bag and went downstairs with her nephew.

They couldn't find Jim Teal in

the library. Miss Mallard aimed her flashlight at an open book.

"Willard, look here!" she said. "This is our family history. But a page has been torn from the book. Obviously, someone does not want us to see a certain name. But whose?"

Then she aimed her flashlight at the floor.

"**Oh, ho!** What's this?" she asked. "It's a basket of garlic! What is it doing *here*?"

"Could it be Cousin Effie's?"

asked Inspector Widgeon.

They left the library. Near the main hall they passed the umbrellas hanging on the rack.

"All fourteen pegs are filled," said Inspector Widgeon, "which means that Cousin Effie and Jim Teal did *not* take their umbrellas and leave."

"So they must be in the castle somewhere," said Miss Mallard.

They went from room to room. Finally they ended up in the cellar, where they saw a closed door.

KISSCULA

Miss Mallard wanted to see what was behind it.

"But aren't you frightened, Aunty?" asked her nephew, shivering.

"Nonsense!" Miss Mallard answered. "I'm an old hand at this. **Come along!**"

Secret Staircases

They opened the door and saw a twisting flight of stairs.

"Follow me, Willard," said Miss Mallard.

They climbed up the narrow, winding stairwell and came to an

abrupt stop before a blank wall.

"Pull that chain hanging from the wall, Willard," commanded Miss Mallard. "Let's see what happens."

Inspector Widgeon took hold of the small chain and pulled. Nothing happened. Then the wall began to swing forward. Suddenly they were in Miss Mallard's room!

"Ugh!" Inspector Widgeon groaned.

He sighed. "I've had enough, Aunty. Relatives disappearing, a

kisspire on the **prowl**, torn pages from a family history, a basket of garlic, secret staircases, cousins I know, and cousins I don't know—**it's all too much**!"

"What did you just say, Willard?" asked Miss Mallard, surprised.

"Never mind," she went on. "I heard you. But remember who you are. Run down and get me that basket of garlic. And bring me a small pan from the kitchen and some cooking oil."

Then she added, "Thanks to what you just said, we are about to catch a **culprit**!"

Inspector Widgeon shook his head and left Miss Mallard's room.

A while later Inspector Widgeon returned with the garlic, the pan, and the oil.

"What is this all about, Aunty?" he asked. "You can't catch a kiss-pire with garlic. **Everyone knows garlic keeps kiss-pires away!**"

"Not this kisspire, Willard," said Miss Mallard. "Now, don't ask me any more questions. We have a lot to do. Please make sure that all the doors and windows of this room are unlocked."

While Inspector Widgeon checked the room, Miss Mallard went to a table and lit a candle. Then she began peeling pieces of garlic.

Ding! Ding! Ding!

The clock struck three. Miss Mallard put the garlic in the pan

OOKING
OIL

with some oil. Then she held the pan over the candle flame. Slowly the strong **aroma** filled the room.

"But, Aunty—" began Inspector Widgeon.

"Quiet, Willard!" whispered Miss Mallard. "Just be on alert for the kisspire."

No sooner had she spoken than the door to the secret entrance slowly opened and someone came into the room.

Inspector Widgeon made a flying leap at the caped intruder.

OOKING
OIL

"Grab him, Willard!" shouted Miss Mallard.

"Kisscula!"

Inspector Widgeon quacked the kisspire's name when he saw who he had pinned to the floor.

"Not Kisscula, Willard," said Miss Mallard as she removed a rubber mask from the intruder's face. "Here is Mario Sprig, the lawyer, disguised as Kisscula. Take him down to the library. I'll get the others. Then I'll explain everything."

6

Kisscula Caught

The first light of dawn was coming through the windows when everyone was finally assembled in the library.

Amy Eider saw Mario Sprig and said, "**It's him!** That's who we saw on our balcony. I can tell by the type of cape he is wearing."

"That's right," said Miss Mallard. "Mario Sprig was pretending to be Count Kisscula. He wanted to frighten us all away so he could keep the castle for himself."

"But how, Aunty?" asked Inspector Widgeon. "Sprig can't inherit the castle. He is not a relative."

"Oh, but he is, Willard!" answered Miss Mallard. "I realized that when you talked about relatives you did not know. Then I remembered the missing page from the family history."

Miss Mallard explained, "It was torn from the book by someone who did not want to be recognized. And that had to be Mario Sprig, because only he did *not* claim to be a relative. I also remembered that you counted fourteen umbrellas. There are only thirteen relatives."

Everyone gasped!

Miss Mallard continued, "That

meant that Sprig had merely pretended to leave the castle. He returned later and replaced his umbrella on the rack."

"But what about the garlic, Aunty?" asked Inspector Widgeon.

"Good question!" Miss Mallard answered. "Everyone knows that some of the best cooking uses garlic. And Mario was on his way to a culinary class in Italy. So I figured a cook would not be able to **resist** its aroma. That's

why I cooked it. I knew he'd come around very quickly."

"The basket!" Inspector Widgeon exclaimed. "It was Mario Sprig's!"

Miss Mallard turned to Mario Sprig and said, "Where are Cousin Effie and Jim Teal? You got rid of them because Cousin Effie recognized you and Jim Teal saw your name in the family history. **Confess**!"

"You win," said Mario Sprig. "Pull the chain beside the fireplace."

When the chain was pulled, the fireplace moved forward, and out came Cousin Effie and Jim Teal, to everyone's joy.

The happy **reunion** lasted through the morning. Then carriages were called to take everyone from Duckinbill Castle.

As Miss Mallard was climbing into a carriage with Inspector Widgeon to take Mario Sprig to jail, she saw a message on the seat. She read the message and showed it to her nephew.

Inspector Widgeon said, **"Who wrote this? Who's playing pranks?"**

"I don't know, Willard," answered Miss Mallard. "But it positively makes me shudder. I can't wait to go somewhere quiet for a spot of tea."

The message said:

Word List

abrupt (a•BRUHPT): Sudden and unexpected

ancient (AYN•chent): Very old

aroma (uh•RO•muh): A nice, pleasant smell

commotion (cuh•MO•shun): Noise and confusion; a noisy disturbance

confess (kun•FESS): To admit as true; to make known

culinary (CUH•luh•nair•ee): Related to food or the kitchen

culprit (KUHL·prit): A person charged with doing something wrong

ear-piercing (EER-PEER·sing): Very loud and irritating to the ear

estate (es·TAYT): Property or money of a person who has passed away

infernal (in·FUR·nul): Extremely unpleasant

inherit (in·HAIR·it): To receive something from a person who has died

knocker (NAH·ker): A ring or bar attached to the outside of a door, used for knocking

prowl (PROWL): To move around in a secret way

resist (ree·ZIST): To stop yourself from doing something you want to do

reunion (ree·YOON·yun): A meeting or gathering of family or friends

revealed (ree·VEELD): Showed clearly

Questions

1. What warning did Great Aunt Abby's will end with?
2. Would you have been afraid to spend the night in the haunted Duckinbill Castle? Why or why not?
3. What do you think the room was like where Effie and Jim Teal were held?
4. Why was Mario Sprig attracted to the aroma of garlic? What food would have attracted you?

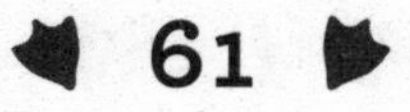

5. What did Miss Mallard take from her knitting bag to help the investigation?

Acknowledgments

My deepest thanks and appreciation go to Jon Anderson, president and publisher of Simon & Schuster Children's Books, and his talented team: Karen Nagel, editor; Karin Paprocki, art director; Tiara Iandiorio, designer; Katherine Devendorf, managing editor; Bernadette Flinn, production manager; Tricia Lin, assistant editor; and Richard Ackoon, executive coordinator;

for launching these incredible editions of my Miss Mallard Mystery books for today's young readers.